11

12

13

14

15

16

17

18

19

20

THE STEPHEN CARTWRIGHT

1 2 3

Philip Hawthorn & Stephen Cartwright

Look out! Look out! For Duck's about,
He's there for you to find.
But when you do, don't count him, too.
(It's all right, he won't mind.)

First published in 1992 by Usborne Publishing Ltd
Usborne House, 83-85 Saffron Hill, London EC1N 8RT.

Illustrations copyright © 1992 Stephen Cartwright
Text copyright © 1992 Philip Hawthorn

The name Usborne and the device
are Trade Marks of Usborne Publishing Ltd.

Printed in Great Britain.

Poor Wiggy Pig is all alone,
A gloomy Number One.
Today's his special birthday tea,
But no one else has come.

Now Pickle Parrot, Number Two,
Squawks loudly as she flies.
"Just hunt around and then you're bound
To get a big surprise."

The kitchen's full of scrummy smells,
But Wiggy mustn't see.
"I'm going to bake a birthday cake,"
Says Walrus, Number Three.

The door bell rings, it's Number Four,
Her smile polite and pleasant.
It's Lady Suzy-Cow who moos,
"My dear, look here, your present."

But Wiggy hears a noise inside,
He screams, "This thing's alive!"
It opens up and out pops Mouse,
A squeaky Number Five.

"I've made you this," says Number Six,
Bel Butterfly by name.
"It's crammed with cream and tastes a dream,
Now aren't you glad I came?"

7

Then Number Seven swings along,
It's Bernadette Baboon.
She's got some grapes and monkey nuts,
And bunches of balloons.

8

"Am I too late?" yells Number Eight,
Who's prancing through the door.
"I've brought some jazz and razzmatazz,"
Says Boogie Dinosaur.

q

Big Baby Hippo, Number Nine,
Has brought some party crackers.
She dances on the table top,
And shakes them like maracas.

10

Then down the chimney Number Ten
Lands softly on her paws.
Miss Sooty Cat says, "Fancy that,
I'm just like Santa Claws."

Eleven's here, Dalmatian Dog,
Who coughs and sniffs and sneezes.
"This pepperoni pizza's topped
With mushrooms, ham and cheeses."

And then they hear a frightened voice
From somewhere in the garden.
It's Kevin Camel, Number Twelve:
"Hello ... I beg your pardon!"

They all look up and see he's stuck
In Wiggy's favourite fir tree.
"I just can't jump because my hump
Is bound to get all dirty."

Oh look! Some bubbles on the pond,
The guests are all agog.
But Wiggy laughs, "It's Myrtle Turtle,
Chatting with a frog."

Then Number Thirteen clambers out,
And says, "How do you do?
I've made some lovely seaweed tea,
And plenty of it, too."

Now Number Fourteen bounces up,
It's Kylie Kangaroo.
"A bonzer birthday, Wig old mate!
Now where's the barbecue?

"I've got a present in my pouch,
For you and all the gang.
It's quite unique, just take a peek:
My famous blue meringue."

Fifteen arrives with two big bowls,
He's looking rather flustered.
"I can't remember which is which,
I think that *this* one's custard."

So Tiger-Tiger dips his paw,
Then yells, "Quick, lemonade!
It's mustard, yike! My tongue's alight,
Please call the fire brigade!"

Sixteen is singing happily,
And dripping on the mat.
It's Davy Crocodile, who sighs,
"I really needed that!

"I've brought some truly t'riffic treats,
The best around, by miles.
They're choc'lates made to look like me,
I call them choc-odiles."

Here's Number Seventeen at last,
It's Elephant Munroe.
"I got quite lost, and then I just
Forgot which way to go.

"But here's some Bubble-ade," he says,
"It fizzles down your spine,
It tweaks your toes and freaks your nose,
At least, it does with mine."

They all go down the cellar steps,
Their tummies rumbling, now.
P.B. the polar bear is there,
Says cool Eighteen, "Like, wow ..."

Inside the freezer sits his gift,
All big and cold and green.
"I know," says Mouse, "it's Wiggy's house,
Made out of mint ice cream."

Nineteen arrives with swoosh of wings,
And breathing flames and fire.
It's Zebedee, who's known to be
The hottest Dragon flier.

He says, "I made some yummy bread,
Although I shouldn't boast.
But then I sneezed, a sizzling breeze,
And turned it into toast."

Lorenzo Lion tumbles in,
And shows them all his tricks.
He juggles mugs and china jugs,
With hard-boiled eggs on sticks.

So Number Twenty takes his place,
The guests are set to eat.
But Wiggy Pig says, "Wait a bit,
There's one more empty seat."

So now it's time to take *your* place,
Before we start the fun.
You too can be at Wiggy's tea,
A special Twenty-one!